GOOD

Magnificent Moon Hare here!

This is Book Two of my fantastic Stuff and
Things. Not Book One or Book Three or
even Book A Million. It's Book Two because
it comes after Book One, as it should, and
not before it, as it shouldn't.

In this book, there are PIRATES, and an
Uncle, and a Budgie, and a Crown, and
lots of Adventures and Stuff that will
make you want to read and read and
not do anything else like go out and visit
Relatives.

You should visit your Relatives though.
That's important to do and there is a
Relative in this book (See above. The
Uncle bit, not the Pirates bit. Unless you
are related to Pirates, which would
be FANTASTIC!)

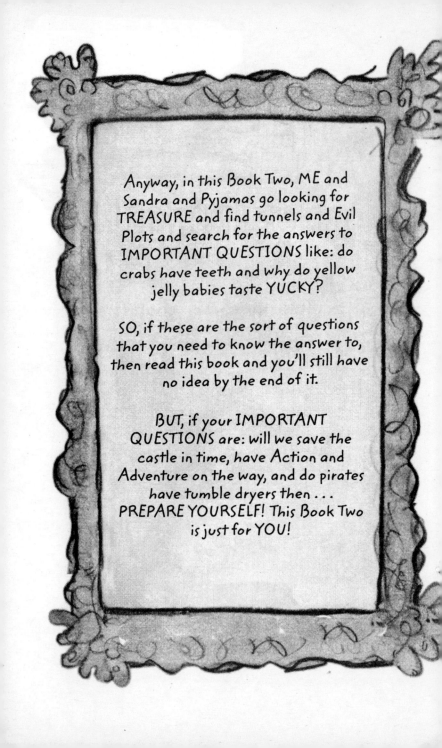

Anyway, in this Book Two, ME and Sandra and Pyjamas go looking for TREASURE and find tunnels and Evil Plots and search for the answers to IMPORTANT QUESTIONS like: do crabs have teeth and why do yellow jelly babies taste YUCKY?

SO, if these are the sort of questions that you need to know the answer to, then read this book and you'll still have no idea by the end of it.

BUT, if your IMPORTANT QUESTIONS are: will we save the castle in time, have Action and Adventure on the way, and do pirates have tumble dryers then . . . PREPARE YOURSELF! This Book Two is just for YOU!

EGMONT

The Magnificent Moon Hare and the Foul Treasure
first published in Great Britain 2012
by Jelly Pie – an imprint of Egmont UK Limited
239 Kensington High Street
London W8 6SA

Text copyright © Sue Monroe 2012
Illustrations copyright © Birgitta Sif 2012

The moral rights of the author and illustrator have been asserted

ISBN 978 1 4052 5876 0

1 3 5 7 9 10 8 6 4 2

A CIP catalogue record for this title is available from the British Library

Printed and bound in Great Britain by the CPI Group

48994/1

EGMONT LUCKY COIN

Our story began over a century ago, when seventeen-year-old Egmont Harald Petersen found a coin in the street.

He was on his way to buy a flyswatter, a small hand-operated printing machine that he then set up in his tiny apartment.

The coin brought him such good luck that today Egmont has offices in over 30 countries around the world. And that lucky coin is still kept at the company's head offices in Denmark.

The Magnificent Moon Hare

and the Foul Treasure

by **SUE MONROE**

Illustrated by **Birgitta Sif**

Jelly Pie

EGMONT

For my mum, Queen Elsie, with
Most Magnificent Love,
Always xx

CONTENTS

Chapter One
PEBBLES AND PIRATES

P.J. Petulant picked up a smooth, wet pebble from the sandy beach of the Little Cove and threw it lazily into the ocean.

'Do you know how long it took for that pebble to get on to the beach?' asked the Moon Hare. 'Its whole life. Now you've just thrown it into the sea and it's got to start ALL OVER again.'

P.J. looked down at the Moon Hare. He was lying on his back on the sand, wearing a rather silly, stripy, all-in-one

bathing suit. His eyes were closed and he had a large blob of green sun block on his nose.

'Stoopid,' said P.J. 'Pebbles don't have lives, they're just pebbles.'

The Moon Hare opened one eye lazily. 'They do too have lives, actually,' he said. 'And names. That one was called Derek.'

'I knew a pebble once,' said Sandra the dragon, joining in. 'It was grey.'

P.J. looked hard at them both.

It hadn't been long since the Moon Hare had returned from the moon to Outlandish, appearing suddenly in the Amazing Maze. Since his return, thought P.J., he had been more harebrained than ever.

P.J. giggled to herself. 'Hare Brained!'

The Moon Hare had his eyes closed again and was humming to himself tunelessly.

Sandra was sitting a little apart from them, further up the beach on his towel. He was wearing an enormous rubber ring around his middle and was staring hard at the sea.

Sandra couldn't swim and he didn't trust the water. 'I don't float,' he would often say to anyone who would listen. 'I glide and I soar, but I don't float. It's not a dragonish thing to do.'

P.J. had learned that there were lots of things that weren't dragonish to do ...

usually because Sandra didn't feel like doing them.

P.J. had learned a lot about Moon Hares too: most importantly, they liked sponge cake with blue icing, wardrobes, stripy tights and 𝒮𝓉𝓊𝒻𝒻. Sometimes she had the feeling that she was the only sensible one in the castle.

Moon Hares could also be great fun but she wouldn't tell him that. Instead she said, 'We should be going back to the castle now, it's nearly teatime and Cook is making beans on toast.'

'And custard,' said the Moon Hare.

'Does the sea look closer, do you think?' asked Sandra suspiciously.

'I used to be a captain on a ship,' said the Moon Hare suddenly.

'They don't have ships on the moon,' said P.J. 'Do you even know what one looks like?'

'I do actually, yes, they are big and wooden and have big white things on them on poles and lots of wool and ladders and bangy pots and a parrot.'

P.J. giggled. 'Silly,' she said.

'They do!' said the Moon Hare sitting up.

'It's definitely getting nearer,' said Sandra, holding his beach towel up for safety.

'Moon Hare, they don't have wool

and bangy pots,' said P.J., standing up and packing her beach towel into her bag.

'They do, and they have a black flappy flag with a smiley face on it.'

'They don't,' said P.J. firmly.

'Do,' said the Moon Hare equally firmly.

'I think that they do, actually,' agreed Sandra.

'Sandra you never go near the sea except when you're with us. And this is a quiet cove, ships just don't come here.'

'What's that then?' asked Sandra, pointing.

P.J. stopped packing and looked out to sea.

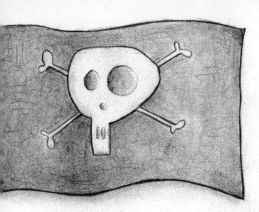

Sure enough, there on the horizon was a ship.

'NERR!' said the Moon Hare rudely, and he stuck out his tongue.

It was a large ship, with billowing white sails. It was painted an unattractive sludge green colour and had shiny brass portholes and yellow masts. At the top of the tallest one flew a very flappy black flag – the Jolly Roger, the flag of a pirate ship.

'Oh dear,' groaned P.J. 'Uncle Julian.'

'What's an u*n*clejulia*n*?' asked the Moon Hare, standing up excitedly.

'Uncle Julian,' said P.J., 'is Mum's brother. They don't get on. Uncle Julian used to be a king just like Dad, but now he's not. Now he's a pirate.'

'Ooh! Lovely!' said the Moon Hare, jumping up and down.

'He's not very piratey,' said P.J. 'He doesn't even have a pirate crew.'

'Oh,' said the Moon Hare and he stopped jumping.

'He must want something; he and Mum always have big arguments. The last time, Mum tried to have his head chopped off.'

10

'OOH! LOVELY!' said the Moon Hare, jumping again.

'But Dad wouldn't let her.'

'Oh,' said the Moon Hare, stopping.

'Mum won't be pleased,' said P.J., picking up her beach mat. 'We had better go and warn her.'

'I will come too,' said Sandra, picking up his beach towel. 'I'm EVER so hot,' he moaned as he followed them towards the castle. 'And I have sand in Places.'

'We are going to meet a Pirate and have FUN AND ADVENTURE AND LOTS OF FANTASTIC STUFF!' said the Moon Hare, standing on one leg. 'The sand will soon fall out of your Places!'

DEREK

Chapter Two
SILVER FOIL AND
SWEETIE WRAPPERS

On reaching the castle they went directly
to the Royal Throne Room.

Queen Elsie was there, sitting in
King Winston's throne as usual. She was
working on a large tapestry that stood on
a frame in front of her, sewing carefully
with a turquoise thread.

'Ah, Petunia!' she said. 'Do come over
here and take a look. I'm doing the family

tapestry again, and I'm having terrible
trouble with your father's ears.'

P.J. took a look.

The tapestry showed the royal family over the years but, as Queen Elsie wasn't particularly good at sewing, it was hard to recognise who was who, mainly because she found sewing heads and hands particularly tricky and so didn't really bother with them.

Queen Elsie stuck out her tongue in concentration and stabbed at the tapestry, stabbing herself in the process.

'If only your father wasn't so difficult . . .' she said, rather unfairly, sucking her stinging finger. 'His side of the family were never very easy to sew. A funny-looking lot if you ask me. You take after my side of the family, dear,' she added, looking at P.J.

'Apart from your ears,' said the Moon Hare.

P.J. scowled at him.

'And your nose,' said the Moon Hare, looking hard at the tapestry.

'Oh, and your –'

'Mum!' interrupted P.J. 'Bad news, I'm afraid. We were on the beach in the Little Cove . . .'

'Oh, dear, poor Sandra,' said Queen Elsie, taking one of Sandra's paws and patting it. 'You don't like the water, do you, dear? Fancy P.J. taking you there. Was it awful?'

15

'Sandy,' said Sandra, looking at the queen slyly under half-lidded eyes. 'The water was very wet and dangerous. It went near to me.'

'Mum . . .'

'You should go and have a lie down, dear,' continued Queen Elsie, fussing over Sandra. 'I'll have a servant bring you some tea and marzipan.'

'That would help,' said Sandra, his eyes glinting wickedly.

'Mum . . .'

'Ooh! Look!' shouted the Moon Hare, still looking at the tapestry. 'Is that Uncle Julian?'

'Uncle who, dear?' asked the queen.

'Uncle Julian! I bet it is! And look, he's having his head chopped off with that big axe!'

'I don't think so, dear,' said the queen, somewhat flustered.

'HE IS!' said the Moon Hare.

'MUM!' bellowed P.J.

'Petunia, don't shout,' said the queen.

'Mum,' whispered P.J. 'Uncle Julian's ship is in the Little Cove.'

'No it isn't, dear,' said the queen. 'Uncle Julian is off somewhere being ridiculous.'

'There's a ship just like Uncle Julian's. It's sludgy green with yellow rigging and . . .'

'Come along, Sandra dear,' said the

queen suddenly. 'Let's see about that tea and marzipan, shall we?'

'Mum, what are we going to do about Uncle Julian?' asked P.J.

'Just ignore him, dear, and he'll go away.'

'He doesn't seem to be going away,' said the Moon Hare a bit later, waving a paw out of the Royal Throne Room window.

'I don't know what all the fuss is about,' said King Winston, joining him. 'I think Julian's rather a splendid fellow,' and he too waved out of the window.

A tall, gangly figure on the beach of the Little Cove waved back.

It was Uncle Julian. He looked very piratey in his red-and-white stripy trousers, a large black belt with a gold buckle, white ruffled shirt and heavy purple coat. On his head he wore a blue felt hat with a yellow feather stuck in it.

He also looked rather wet.

They could see his pirate ship anchored out to sea and Uncle Julian was tugging at a small rowing boat, trying to pull it on to the beach.

He was having some trouble, slipping and sliding in the water as the small rowing boat, which seemed to have a mind of its own, fought against him, twisting and turning and threatening to flip upside down.

After they had watched this for a little while, they moved away from the window, just as the rowing boat dragged Uncle Julian down the beach and back into the sea.

The Moon Hare was very excited at the thought of meeting a pirate. He was dressed for the occasion, wearing a long red jacket with gold braid on the lapels, that he had 'found' in one of the servants' rooms, his green stripy tights and two large silver curtain rings taken from P.J.'s bedroom curtains, dangling from his long ears. He had also made himself a telescope from three toilet roll middles.

He was very careful to take all of the toilet paper off them first, making sure that he stuffed it tidily away down the toilet.

'What do you think he wants?' asked P.J., who had quickly grown bored of watching her uncle and was sitting upside down on King Winston's throne, her head dangling down to the floor, and her legs up in the air. She was casually kicking the back of the seat.

'Who knows,' said her father, sitting on the queen's throne. 'Last we heard from him was that postcard he sent from Australia.'

'Ooh! Australia!' said the Moon Hare. 'He's EXOTIC!'

'Mum thinks he's annoying,' said P.J.

At that moment, the doors to the Throne Room swung open and in walked

Queen Elsie. She was dressed in full ceremonial robes and was wearing her favourite, largest crown, which she kept for special occasions.

It was trimmed with the softest fake fur and covered in diamonds, rubies and emeralds.

'Ooh!' said the Moon Hare, making some room in his stripy tights. 'Nice crown, Your Elsiness, I especially like the sweetie wrappers. Shall I look after it for you?'

'No thank you, dear,' said Queen Elsie.

'What sweetie wrappers?' asked P.J.

'On my crown, dear,' said the queen. 'The diamond is missing, I don't think

that you can tell, at least not
if you don't look too closely.'

P.J., who had never really
taken much notice of her
mother's royal crown before,
looked hard at it now.

Sure enough, there in
the centre of it was a
lump of tin foil and some sweet wrappers.

'Where's the real diamond?' asked
P.J. in surprise.

'Do you mean the large and incredibly
priceless Petulant Diamond, dear? I have
no idea; it's been lost for a very long time.'

'I suspect King Rupert,' said King
Winston in a whispered voice. 'He's never

quite recovered from when I cunningly foiled his plot to have me beheaded. Things go missing around here all the time.'

P.J. looked at the Moon Hare, who looked back at her innocently.

'**SERVANT!**' Queen Elsie bellowed, making everyone take a small step backwards.

A servant arrived in the doorway, bowing low. He looked very flustered and red in the face, and was carrying a toilet plunger in one hand.

He was wearing a footman's jacket that was two sizes too big for him and, as he stood up, the jacket slipped down

from his shoulders and on to the floor, revealing a rather grey-looking vest underneath.

'Sorry, sorry, Your Highnesses,' he muttered, pulling it back up and turning even redder. 'I was rather delayed in my quarters.'

He caught sight of the Moon Hare and stopped for a moment, looking at him oddly.

The Moon Hare peered back through his toilet roll telescope.

'Go and fetch Julian, that awfully annoying man on the beach,' said Queen Elsie tetchily. 'Tie up his ridiculous little rowing boat and **BRING HIM**

TO ME.'

The servant nodded, leaving quickly. He had never seen the queen so cross before.

'Ooh!' said the Moon Hare, 'Your Elsiness, I do like it when you BIG UP your voice like that.'

'Thank you, dear,' said the queen.

'Um, Elsie my love,' began the king anxiously. 'Be honest now, you don't have the royal executioner standing by do you?'

'Possibly,' said the queen, not meeting his eye. 'We will just have to see what Julian has to say for himself. My throne please, Winston, and P.J., dear, do sit like a lady.'

27

'I am,' said P.J. untruthfully, waving with her foot.

'PETUNIA!' shouted the queen.

P.J. jumped, sliding off the throne and on to the floor in a heap.

'That's better dear, thank you,' said the queen, sitting on her throne and smoothing down her royal robes. 'I'm ready now.'

'SO AM I!' said the Moon Hare suddenly, standing on his head.

'What are you doing?' asked P.J.

'Making Uncle Julian feel at home,' said the Moon Hare. 'Everybody knows that from here, Australia is upside down.'

Chapter Three
FOUL JELLY BABIES

There came a knock at the Royal Throne Room doors, they opened and the servant – who was now somewhat wetter and more bedraggled than before – entered, followed by Uncle Julian.

'The Uncle Julian, Your Majesty,' said the servant, sniffing loudly. 'I found him in the sea.' He bowed low, making little rivers of water on the floor, before squelching out of the room.

Uncle Julian looked miserable. His

white ruffled shirt was no longer ruffly and the pockets of his heavy purple coat were full of seawater. He had lost his shoes and his grey frizzy hair was plastered to his head, while the blue felt hat now hung limply over his ears, its yellow feather sagging sadly.

On his shoulder, looking bored, was

a very small bony bird. It stood about ten centimetres tall and had blue and red, rather oily-looking feathers and a yellow crest.

P.J. looked at it. It looked nothing like the fine parrots that the pirates in her books wore on their shoulders. There was something about it that wasn't at all nice, she decided.

The bird scowled back at her with beady black eyes.

'G'day, Uncle Julian!' said the Moon Hare, still upside down. 'AHOY and all that! WHAT HO, ME KANGAROO!'

'Pardon?' said Uncle Julian.

'Yo-Ho-Ho! Hoist the

31

mainsail!' continued the Moon Hare, jumping up the right way.

'Hello, Uncle Julian,' said P.J., getting up to give her uncle a hug.

'Hello, pet!' said Uncle Julian, returning the hug rather wetly.

The small bird pecked Uncle Julian sharply on the neck.

'OWW!' Sorry,' said Uncle Julian, wincing.

'Do you have a wooden leg?' asked the Moon Hare rudely. 'Can I kick you and see?' He took aim.

'No, Moon Hare!' said P.J. quickly. 'Uncle Julian doesn't have a wooden leg ... Do you?' she asked hopefully.

'No. Sorry,' replied Uncle Julian.

'Who's your budgie?' asked the Moon Hare excitedly, pointing to the bird.

The bird pecked Uncle Julian again.

'OWW!' Sorry,' said Uncle Julian, rubbing his sore neck. 'This is Foul, he's my advisor and companion.'

'Julian, my dear fellow!' said King Winston stepping forward and shaking Uncle Julian's hand. 'Been a long time ...' King Winston looked at his wife. Queen Elsie was as still as a statue on her throne. 'Yes, too long . . . Isn't that right, dear?' continued the king hurriedly to fill the gap. 'Why, Julian, Elsie and I were only saying the other day that it's been too long . . . Too long . . .' He looked to the queen for help.

Queen Elsie stayed where she was, staring hard at Uncle Julian.

'Hello, Else!' said Uncle Julian brightly.

Peck! Foul nipped his neck.

'*OWW!*' said Uncle Julian, looking miserable again.

Queen Elsie turned to King Winston. 'Tell Julian that he should go to the guest quarters and change out of his ridiculous pirate clothes and into something more regal,' she said, using her best royal voice. 'He will find something in the wardrobe. We will meet with him here in exactly one hour.'

King Winston looked at Uncle Julian.

'Umm . . .' he began.

'I heard,' said Uncle Julian stiffly. 'That sounds like a good idea to me. I will return in about an hour.'

The queen flinched. 'One hour, Winston,' said Queen Elsie.

'Um . . .' said King Winston.

'One hour and ten,' said Uncle Julian.

Foul sniggered unpleasantly.

'Come along, Uncle Julian,' said P.J. quickly. 'I will show you the way.'

P.J. led Uncle Julian from the Throne Room, followed by the Moon Hare, who was still asking questions.

'When you are on your boat . . .'

'Ship,' corrected Uncle Julian.

'Yes. When you are on your boat, do you have a treasure chest? I have stripy tights, they are roomier than they look,' continued the Moon Hare, twanging his tights as he bounced.

P.J. couldn't be sure but she thought she saw Foul lean forward as if to peck the Moon Hare. The Moon Hare didn't notice but carried on with his questions.

'Do you have a parrot on your boat?' he asked.

This time she was sure that Foul tried to.

'When you're on your boat,' said the

Moon Hare, still jumping around the bewildered Uncle Julian, 'do you shiver your timbers?'

'Are we nearly there?' Uncle Julian asked P.J.

'Yes we are,' she replied, trying not to giggle. 'In fact, it's right here.'

They stopped outside the guest bedroom.

'Good luck with Mum,' said P.J. 'I've never seen her so cross and I make her cross loads.'

'Thank you. *OWW!*' said Uncle Julian after another peck from Foul. 'Sorry . . .' As he walked through the door Foul looked back over his shoulder. The

glare that he gave them made P.J. shiver.

'I don't think that I like that Foul,' she said to the Moon Hare, as they headed out to the castle grounds 'He keeps pecking poor Uncle Julian.'

'OWW! Sorry!' said the Moon Hare.

'That bird's definitely NOT to be trusted,' said P.J.

'Really?' said the Moon Hare. 'Maybe he's just shy. I will be EXTRA friendly to him, he will like that.'

P.J. doubted that he would.

A little while later, the Moon Hare was sitting on P.J.'s bed eating jelly babies,

occasionally spitting a yellow one back into the bag.

'Stop it!' said P.J. as he missed the bag and hit her duvet cover.

'I don't like the yellow ones,' replied the Moon Hare in a sticky voice. Then jumping up he said, 'Let's go and see the dragon.'

'What, now?' said P.J. 'It's nearly bedtime and I've just put on my pyjamas.'

'Yes, I am in a Sandra sort of mood,' said the Moon Hare casually. 'I am often in the mood for a dragon.'

'Even a dragon like Sandra?' said P.J., thinking that sometimes Sandra was just a bit weird.

'Never underestimate a dragon,' said the Moon Hare, spitting out another sweet. 'You do so at your own risk.'

'OK then,' said P.J. with a sigh and she pulled on her dressing gown.

The Moon Hare was still in his pirate costume.

'Are you ever going to take that off?' she asked him.

'NOPE!' he said, and clutching his bag of jelly babies he hopped out of the door.

When they reached Sandra's apartments on the top floor of the tower, they found that he was not in.

'Pants,' said the Moon Hare, sitting

on the doorstep. 'We will just have to wait.'

He put another jelly baby into his mouth, before rummaging around in his green stripy tights and producing a dog-eared crossword puzzle book and a yellow HB pencil. Then he began to write quick, random letters in the little boxes.

'You are not doing that right,' said P.J., sitting next to him and looking over his shoulder. 'You have to follow the clues.'

'Don't,' said the Moon Hare slurping as he wrote. 'Ah!' he said, 'that's a W, I like Ws. They are my favourite number.'

'A W isn't a number,' corrected P.J. 'And the clue for that word is: "Unexpected visitor".'

'Yes, W,' said the Moon Hare stubbornly.

'You can't just write Ws in all of the boxes.'

'Can,' said the Moon Hare. 'Look!' And he quickly scrawled a W in every box.

'The answer is "Whale",' said Sandra, appearing suddenly.

'Ah! Of course, thank you,' said the Moon Hare, writing another W.

'That's not right!' P.J. spluttered.

42

'Yes it is,' said Sandra. 'A whale would be a very unexpected visitor.'

'Unless you were in the bath,' added the Moon Hare.

'Of course,' agreed Sandra, unlocking his room with a large golden key.

They followed him in.

'Where have you been?' asked P.J.

'Nowhere,' said Sandra.

'Where have you been?' asked the Moon Hare.

Sandra took a deep breath. 'Well, Aunty Elsie asked me to go to the meeting with Uncle Julian to make him ANXIOUS and it worked because he was and I think that there is going to

be trouble because Uncle Julian had something very exciting and now some other pirates have it and Aunty Elsie is very worried and is talking about battle plans although I don't know what they are because I was busy not listening.'

'Why didn't you tell **ME** that?' said P.J. huffily.

'You didn't ask,' replied the dragon.

'Anything else?' asked P.J.

'No.'

'Anything else?' asked the Moon Hare.

'Only that Aunty Elsie threatened to chop off Uncle Julian's head because he's annoyed her which would be splendid but Aunty Elsie can't chop his head off

because King Winston has given the executioner a SUDDEN HOLIDAY which has made Aunty Elsie REALLY cross.'

Sandra let out his breath with a WHOOSH! And sat down on his bed, inspecting his talons.

'Stoopid,' muttered P.J. crossly, folding her arms.

'We must find out what the exciting THING is!' said the Moon Hare jumping up and down. 'I bet that it's TREASURE! That's what us Pirates love. We can ask Uncle Julian where the treasure is and then we can have it!'

'What will we do with it?' asked Sandra,

who didn't much care for treasure.

'I will look after it in my secret place.'

'Your green stripy tights,' said P.J.

The Moon Hare gave her A Look.

'In my SECRET PLACE,' he repeated. 'Until we can decide.'

'Well, we had better get going,' said Sandra. 'I think that Aunty Elsie will find another executioner soon or, if not, she'll do it herself.'

'What about that Foul creature?' asked P.J. 'I don't like him; I bet he's up to something.'

'I will distract him,' said the Moon Hare. 'I'm good at that.' And he spat another jelly baby back into the bag.

P.J. opened the door. She couldn't be sure but she thought that she saw something out of the corner of her eye, moving, almost fluttering, in the corridor.

'That's Foul,' she said.

'Sorry!' said the Moon Hare and as he hopped past he took the soggy yellow jelly babies out of the bag and squished them into her hand instead.

Chapter Four
RETURN OF THE PIRATES!

When they reached Uncle Julian's room, the Moon Hare had to hammer extra loudly on the door until he answered.

Although it was early in the evening, Uncle Julian had clearly been asleep in bed. They could tell, as he was wearing a nightshirt and spotty blue nightcap and his face looked like it needed ironing.

He seemed puzzled to see them.

'Hello, Uncle Julian,' said P.J. in an innocent voice. 'We thought that we would come for a visit.'

'Do you have any sponge cake?' asked the Moon Hare, rushing past Uncle Julian into the room.

'Or marzipan?' asked Sandra, hopefully, following him.

'Ook! Hello, Budgie!' said the Moon Hare.

Foul was perched on the bedpost. He glared at the Moon Hare who beamed

back at him.

P.J. wondered how much of their conversation Foul had overheard from outside Sandra's room.

'I have brought you a present,' said the Moon Hare to Foul, who was edging away from him along the headboard. 'Look! It's a lovely bell for your budgie cage!' And he produced an enormous golden bell from his stripy tights.

He shook it energetically.

BONG! BONG! BONG!

They all covered their ears with their hands.

'Foul doesn't have a cage,' shouted Uncle Julian over the noise. 'He is not that sort of bird.'

'Oh, that's a bit of luck!' said the Moon Hare, putting down the bell and reaching into his tights again. 'I have one that's perfect for him!' And he produced a miniature ornate silver cage, with a small swing and a mirror in it.

'YARK!' said an outraged Foul.

As the Moon Hare went to grab him, Foul fluttered to the top of the wardrobe.

'I think that he likes it,' said the Moon Hare, jumping on to the bed to reach him.

'I'll open the door and he can just fly in.'

'I'll help,' offered Sandra, and he took a swipe at Foul, who tried to peck him.

'Uncle Julian,' began P.J., sensing that now was her moment. 'Can I talk to you about something?' She tugged at Uncle Julian's nightshirt to get his attention away from the activity on the other side of the room.

'Umm . . . Yes, dear?' said Uncle Julian who was still somewhat distracted.

'Uncle Julian, what is it that the pirates have that has made mum so cross? Is it treasure? Are you in danger and can we help?'

She thought she had best get it out

quickly before Foul attacked the Moon
Hare and got eaten by Sandra.

Uncle Julian looked at her.

'How did you know about that? Oh,
of course, the dragon told you,' he said.
'Well it's nothing to worry about, pet.'

He patted her on the head.

P.J. could sense that she was running
out of time. Foul was on the curtains
now, trying desperately to peck the Moon
Hare, who was jumping up and down
and waving the cage at him, while Sandra
was busy unhooking the curtains from
the curtain pole.

P.J. did what she knew would work.
It had worked with her parents, with

the nannies, with anyone who had ever said 'no' to her. She sat on the carpet and began to cry.

It went well. Uncle Julian stopped paying any attention to the chaos taking place at the window and bent down to P.J. 'Now, now, what's all this?' he asked kindly.

'I jus . . . jus . . . wanted to . . . know,' blubbed P.J., 'whe . . . where the . . . treasure is . . . that's . . . all . . .'

'But I don't know, my pet,' said Uncle Julian.

'WHAA!'

bawled P.J.

'P.J., my pet,' said Uncle Julian, getting really concerned. 'I don't know where the treasure is, but I can tell you what the pirates have.'

P.J. stopped crying immediately.

'So it is treasure? What have the pirates got?' she asked.

SNAP!

The door to the budgie cage was shut tightly, with an enraged Foul trapped inside.

'There!' said the Moon Hare brightly. 'How lovely, he REALLY likes it, Uncle Julian.'

Foul didn't look like he was really liking it.

Even though he was a small bird, he was still larger than the tiny bird cage and he couldn't move a feather. He could

scowl at them though, and he did so through the bars of the cage.

'Now, Sandra will take him for a little walk, so that he may partake of the evening air,' said the Moon Hare, stepping over the broken curtain pole and tattered curtains, and giving the cage to Sandra.

The cage struggled.

'Yes!' said Sandra, in a falsely bright voice. 'Come along, Foul, let us partake.'

And he took the furious Foul out of the room.

P.J. blinked up at Uncle Julian.

She sniffed loudly. 'Well?' she asked.

Uncle Julian hesitated.

P.J.'s bottom lip began to tremble.

'All right!' said Uncle Julian. 'I will tell you, P.J., if you promise not to cry again.'

'She promises,' said the Moon Hare, joining P.J. on the carpet and looking up at Uncle Julian. with large round eyes.

'Oh, well, I suppose it will be all right,' said Uncle Julian 'You see I sort of *own* a map. I've had it forever and now some other pirates have it . . . I don't think that Foul meant to give it to them . . . He said that he did it accidentally.'

'I bet he didn't do it accidentally,' said P.J.

'Accidents happen, pet. Anyway, here's the interesting part. I always knew that

it was a treasure map, but what I didn't realise until now is that this castle is marked on it. It was Foul who spotted that. He's very clever and useful, you know.'

'Which is why I gave him that nice cage,' said the Moon Hare.

'Oh, Uncle Julian,' said P.J. in despair. 'So these pirates think that there is treasure hidden somewhere around or in this castle, they have a map to follow and they're on their way to follow it! What can we do?' She felt like crying for real now.

Uncle Julian looked thoughtful.

'Well, I could draw it, I suppose,' he said. 'Then we would have one too.'

'What?' said P.J.

'I said, I could draw it, I suppose,' repeated Uncle Julian. 'You see, I carried it about for so long that I know every detail, pet.'

The Moon Hare stood up and reached inside his stripy tights. He produced a sheet of paper and some felt-tipped pens.

'Go on then!' he said, handing them to Uncle Julian.

Uncle Julian sat on the floor and took the lids off the pens.

'One at a time, Uncle Julian, or you'll stain the carpet,' said P.J. sensibly.

'But I need all the colours,' whined Uncle Julian.

'I will hold them for you,' said P.J., and she picked up the pens.

Uncle Julian began to draw. He stuck out his tongue as he worked, trying very hard to remember every detail.

The Moon Hare insisted on joining in.

'But you don't know the map,' said P.J. 'It needs to be accurate, Moon Hare!'

The Moon Hare held on tightly to his felt-tip.

'He can colour the trees,' said Uncle Julian kindly.

'And the river,' said the Moon Hare. 'And the sun.'

'There isn't a sun. It's a map,' said P.J.

'Sun!' said the Moon Hare and he

drew a large sun in the corner of the picture, wearing a pair of sunglasses.

It took a long time, but finally the map was almost finished.

Uncle Julian chewed the end of his felt-tip and thought hard. 'I hope that I've not missed anything out,' he said, admiring his artwork.

The Moon Hare was busy finishing off a banana that he had added next to the large letter **X** that marked the spot.

The spot where the treasure was buried.

P.J. noticed that he had also added a train, a sports car and something that looked like a cross between a zebra and

an elephant.

'I think that we should stop now,' said P.J., picking up the paper and rolling it up.

Suddenly, Sandra entered, without the bird cage and looking very bad tempered.

'Where is Foul?' asked Uncle Julian.

'I lost him,' snapped Sandra.

'Sandra, you haven't eaten him, have you?' asked P.J., secretly hoping that he had.

'Absolutely not!' said Sandra. 'Horrid little oily thing. I just can't remember where I left him, that's all.'

'Is he still in his cage?' asked Uncle Julian in alarm.

'Yes,' said Sandra. 'Only I opened

the door a little so that he could see the interesting thing that I was trying to show him and he bit me, so I sort of accidentally dropped him.'

'What was the interesting thing?' asked the Moon Hare.

'It was the other pirate ship,' said the dragon. 'We went to the Little Cove to see it because it is there, although we didn't go near the nasty wet water.'

'You dropped him in the Little Cove?' asked Uncle Julian, hoping that the tide had not come in.

'No,' said Sandra, 'it was after that, on the way back towards the castle kitchens. He kept sniggering in an unpleasant way

and when I asked him why, he wouldn't say and just sniggered again. Very rude. I may have accidentally lost him in one of the kitchen dustbins.'

'I had better go and rescue him!' squeaked Uncle Julian anxiously, slipping his coat on over his nightshirt.

P.J. suddenly realised what Sandra had said. 'Did you say *another* pirate ship is here?' she asked.

'Yes,' replied Sandra. 'They have a smart blue ship. The pirates are on your ship too now, Uncle Julian. That means that you won't be on your own any more, which is nice.'

Uncle Julian turned pale.

'Look out of the window,' said Sandra. 'You'll see them.'

They all crowded around the window. Another pirate ship could now be seen bobbing on the sea close to Uncle Julian's. There was a lot of activity on-board his ship. The pirates were throwing things off it: a chair, table and a bookcase flew through the air to land with a SPLASH! in the sea.

'They're making a terrible mess,' said P.J. 'Mum will be furious.'

'My clothes!' shouted Uncle Julian as shirts, trousers and shoes were thrown overboard.

Stop It! he yelled out of

the window.

SPLASH! went the wardrobe, following its contents into the sea. Numerous pairs of underwear – some spotty, some plain and some stripy – floated gently to the surface.

'That's pants, Uncle Julian!' said the Moon Hare.

'Come on!' said P.J., rushing to the door. 'We had better find the treasure before those pirates do!'

Chapter Five
PLANS AND PICNICS

'This way!' shouted P.J. as they raced along the corridor. 'The map starts at the Throne Room!'

'All right then!' yelled the Moon Hare, and changed directions.

He did so suddenly, making P.J. trip up. She rubbed her sore knee and gave him A Look.

'It's this way,' she said, pointing down the corridor.

'Then why did you stop?' asked the

Moon Hare. 'We were going that way in the first place.'

'Going anywhere with you takes such a long time as you are always tripping up,' said Sandra to P.J.

'Perhaps your ears are unbalanced,' said the Moon Hare. 'I have heard that it can make you trip, if one of your ears is higher than the other.'

'Especially if they are on the large side, as yours are,' said Sandra.

'Which side is the large side?' asked the Moon Hare.

'The left,' replied Sandra.

'Stoopid,' said P.J., but she felt her ears

when the others weren't looking.

When they reached the Royal Throne Room they opened the doors and went inside.

Queen Elsie was pacing up and down, looking worried.

She was no longer wearing her best royal clothes and splendid royal crown. Instead, she was dressed for bed, wearing a flannelette nightdress and pink slippers with bunny ears on them. Her hair was covered in wobbly curlers which bounced up and down as she walked.

King Winston was sitting on his throne watching her. He was also dressed for bed, wearing a blue dressing gown

with orange silk pyjamas underneath, red woolly slippers and a green night cap with a tassel on it.

'Ah, P.J., my dove,' he said. 'Good to see you.' He lowered his voice. 'Have you seen the mess in the Little Cove?'

'Yes! And the pirates have got Uncle Julian's treasure map!' said P.J.

'Typical of Julian,' hissed Queen Elsie. 'Where is he anyway?'

'He's gone to find Foul,' said P.J. 'Sandra accidentally lost him.'

Sandra smiled and blew a casual smoke ring into the air.

'Its very exciting, isn't it?' said the Moon Hare, jumping up and down.

'I LOVE PIRATES!'

'ANYWAY,' said P.J., thinking that the Moon Hare hadn't quite grasped how dangerous the situation was. 'Uncle Julian has drawn a copy of the map from his memory which I think is really rather clever.'

'CLEVER!' screeched the queen.

'Now, dear,' said the king, standing up, 'remember to breathe.'

'Look, Your Elsiness!' said the Moon Hare, reaching into his stripy tights. 'Here it is, and it's very fantastic – especially the racing car.'

'Oh, yes,' said the king, looking at the paper. 'A Lamborghini, isn't it? And that's a lovely stripy elephant.'

Queen Elsie slumped on to her throne, holding her hand to her throbbing head.

'Look!' said the king, really enjoying himself. 'That green scribbly bit looks just like the royal maze.'

'Let me see,' said P.J., leaning in to take a look. 'It is the maze, you're right! That's where we should go next!'

'Come along, let's go *NOW!*' yelled the Moon Hare eagerly. 'And we can take sponge cake!'

'I will instruct Cook to get up and make a picnic hamper!' said King Winston happily.

Queen Elsie stood up. 'Is no one

worried about the pirate ship waiting to attack the castle? Or is that just me?' she asked.

'That's why we need to get to the treasure first, before they do, and then we can bargain with them,' said P.J.

'Lovely!' said the queen, slumping back down again. 'Bargaining with a bunch of dastardly pirates – why not? Maybe we should ask Cook to make them up a picnic hamper too?'

'I think that Sandra should stay here with you,' said P.J. kindly. 'That way he can keep you safe.'

'Good idea,' said Sandra. 'I would like to stay here with my Aunty Elsie.'

He took Queen Elsie's hand and stroked it. 'Perhaps we could ask Cook to find some Safety Marzipan?' Queen Elsie nodded. 'And if you read me a bedtime story, that would make you Feel Safer too,' he added slyly.

Just then, Uncle Julian entered the throne room.

Foul was perched on his shoulder, looking very dirty. His usually oily feathers were now matted together and he smelled of rotten eggs.

'POOEY!' said the Moon Hare.

Foul glared at the Moon Hare, who waved a paw in his direction, and snarled at Sandra, who totally ignored him.

'*OWW!* Sorry,' said Uncle Julian after a peck. 'It's all right, you can stop worrying now, I've found Foul.' The others looked at him blankly. 'Apparently it's dustbin day tomorrow and so the kitchen boy had wheeled his wheelie bin out on to the castle drive . . .'

'Oh, good,' said the queen. 'I meant to remind the kitchen staff to do that.'

'I arrived only just in time!' said Uncle Julian, scowling at the queen.

'Well, Julian, we have your splendid map here,' said King Winston, 'and I must say it's awfully good. We've worked out the first clue already.'

P.J. noticed Foul look surprised at

this for a moment and then sit up and pay close attention, his beady black eyes scanning the map.

'Yes! We are going into the outside garden to the Amazing Maze with torches and cake!' said the Moon Hare to Uncle Julian. 'You may come too, little Budgie!'

P.J. thought that Foul looked pleased, if such a thing were possible.

'We need to get a move on!' she said.

'Let's meet up in the Royal Hall in ten minutes,' said King Winston.

'Good idea,' said Uncle Julian. 'Make sure you look after my map.'

'It's safe,' said the Moon Hare, taking the map from King Winston and putting

it into his stripy tights. 'No one would
EVER look in there.'

P.J. thought that he was probably right.

Chapter Six
THE AMAZING MAZE'S
NIGHT TIME WAYS

Ten minutes had passed and so had another fifteen by the time they all finally arrived.

P.J. was pacing up and down impatiently. She had changed into her jeans and a blue jumper and she had still been on time, even though the Moon Hare had suddenly decided to accessorise his outfit by adding a large black hat with

an enormous peacock feather attached to it, a yellow plastic cutlass and an eye patch.

P.J. had insisted that he wore the patch in the middle of his forehead instead of over his eye, after he had knocked over a bookcase and fallen down a flight of stairs on their brief journey from her room to the Royal Hall.

Uncle Julian arrived next, wearing his pirate clothes. They had been washed and ironed and the ruffles on his shirt neatly starched. Foul, as usual, was with him, looking oddly smug and self-satisfied.

They were about to give up on King Winston when he arrived, still wearing his night clothes, out of breath and carrying a large picnic hamper, four torches, a table cloth, a small folding table, matching chairs and a badminton set.

'Dad! You're late!' said P.J. crossly. 'And you can't take all of that with you!'

'But I thought that we would make an evening of it,' said the king.

'We are trying to save the castle, Dad. You will have to leave it here,' said P.J. firmly.

'Take the torches!' said Uncle Julian.

'And the hamper!' said the Moon Hare.

'Leave the rest,' said P.J.

King Winston did as he was told, leaving the unwanted things next to the suit of armour, and they made their way out of the castle towards the Amazing Maze.

The Moon Hare bounced in front, leading the way.

It was a still, warm summer night and hundreds of stars lit up the velvet night sky.

The moon was a beautiful silver sliver.

The Moon Hare bowed low to it. 'Good greetings!' he said, and the stars twinkled.

They wound their way along the gravel path until they came to the entrance to the maze.

'Let's look at the map,' said P.J.

The Moon Hare pulled the now rather crumpled paper from his stripy tights and unrolled it.

'It looks like we shall have to go all the way into the centre,' said P.J. 'I wonder why? I've been there **HUNDREDS** of times and I've never seen anything that looks like treasure.'

P.J. led the way into the Amazing Maze.

It was a lot cooler inside and the large, dense hedges felt a hundred feet high.

They turned their torches on but that didn't make a lot of difference. Nothing seemed to break through the heavy darkness.

P.J. wasn't sure that she liked the maze at night.

In the day it was fun, a sea of green stretching out as far as the eye could see. However, here at night the maze was full of rustling, creaking sounds. The maze seemed to affect the others too. King Winston and Uncle Julian

stayed close together, walking without a sound. Even Foul seemed bothered by it, looking around anxiously.

Only the Moon Hare was completely undisturbed by the maze and its night time ways. He bounced on ahead, then behind, then ahead again, making a lot of noise.

'BOING! BOING! THE AMAZING MAZE!' he shouted, jumping up and down.

'Sssh, Moon Hare!' said P.J.

'BOING! BOING!' shouted the Moon Hare, disappearing round a bend.

After plodding on in darkness, losing all sense of time and their bearings, they suddenly came to a halt in the centre of the maze. The Moon Hare was nowhere to be seen.

'Well,' said Uncle Julian, in almost a whisper. 'Here we are then. Now what?'

They shone their torches into the gloom, their dim lights landing on the hedges and the stone bench in the centre of the clearing.

'BOING!' shouted the Moon Hare, bouncing out from a hedge and making

everyone jump.

'Moon Hare!' hissed P.J. 'Be quiet and help us look around for clues.'

'I'm tired,' said Uncle Julian, sitting down on the bench. 'Shall we open the hamper?'

'Ooh! Yes!' squeaked the Moon Hare excitedly.

'Here it is,' said King Winston, and he sat down next to Uncle Julian and opened up the basket.

'Not yet,' said P.J. 'We need to look at the map again. Moon Hare, bring it over here and I'll shine my torch on it.'

The Moon Hare produced the map and P.J. looked at it with him as best

they could in the poor light.

CLUNK!

'What was that?' squeaked P.J.

They turned around quickly, shining their torches towards the loud noise. There was nothing to be seen. Just the empty stone bench, with the picnic hamper standing next to it, left open and untouched.

'Dad?' P.J. took a step towards it. 'Uncle Julian?' She shone her torch around the hedges.

'What could have happened to them?' asked P.J. nervously.

'EVIL BUDGIE WHERE ARE YOU?!' bellowed the Moon Hare.

'They were here!' said P.J. walking over to the bench and sitting down.

CLUNK!

P.J. disappeared.

'THAT WAS BRILLIANT!' shouted the Moon Hare. 'DO IT AGAIN!'

Then, realising that there was no one else to do it except him, the Moon Hare picked up a piece of sponge cake with blue icing from the picnic basket and sat on the stone bench.

CLUNK!

It tilted backwards very suddenly and the Moon Hare was flung down into a dark hole below.

'WHEE!' he shouted.

He slid for a while until he landed with a **THWUMP!** on top of P.J. This annoyed her as she had just picked herself up.

They had fallen into an underground tunnel. It was a very bright tunnel, lit by wall lights with frilly lampshades and candle-shaped bulbs. When they took a closer look, they saw that the walls were papered with yellow-embossed wallpaper.

'Feels velvety,' said the Moon Hare, stroking it.

As they walked along, the Moon Hare ate his sponge cake, dropping crumbs on the soft, thick, lime-green carpet.

'You are making a terrible mess,' said P.J.

'Sthorwy,' said the Moon Hare, splattering her with cake and icing.

'Just stop eating,' said P.J. crossly, wiping herself down. 'Give me the cake.' And she put her hand out.

The Moon Hare looked at her and quickly stuffed the last, enormous piece of cake into his mouth.

'Moon Hare!'

'YAAAR!' The Moon Hare opened his mouth wide to reveal a soggy, chewed mess.

'That's revolting,' said P.J.

His cheeks bulging, he swallowed it quickly.

'HIC!' he said.

P.J. gave him A Look and carried on walking.

'HIC!'

'Someone has taken a lot of time decorating this tunnel,' said P.J. 'I wonder who it was and where the tunnel leads?'

The tunnel twisted and turned and began to widen out. In this part of it, objects had been arranged in a deliberate way, on shelves and on the floor. Strange, mismatched things: a boomerang, a pair of green wellington boots and a straw donkey with bulging eyes.

'Whoever it was, they're brilliant at it!' the Moon Hare said. 'HIC! If I had a tunnel, I would like it to be just like this one. 𝓗𝐼𝐶!' And he stroked the walls some more with his sticky paws as he walked.

P.J. didn't agree. The colours in the tunnel hurt her eyes and the objects that were on display were awful.

Small unidentifiable creatures made from shells were lined up regimentally on shelves, along with a plastic lobster and a red London double-decker bus.

The tunnel turned to the left and in front of them was a flight of stairs.

'Come along, Moon Hare,' said P.J. 'Up we go!'

'𝔂𝖊𝓪𝔂! 𝐔𝐏!' said the Moon Hare, hopping up the stairs two at a time. '𝓗𝐼𝐶!'

It didn't take them long to reach the top,

where they stopped at a door in the wall.

It was a big red door and it was slightly ajar, as if someone had recently gone through it.

P.J. hoped that it had been King Winston and Uncle Julian, because as yet, there had been no sign of them and that was beginning to worry her. She pushed the door open and, followed by the Moon Hare, she stepped through.

They found themselves, to their surprise, in a familiar place.

'Hello!' said King Winston cheerily. 'Isn't it funny, we've ended up in Sandra's room!'

Chapter Seven
UNCLE JULIAN'S SECRET

'Why would Sandra have a secret tunnel?' asked P.J. sitting herself down on the bed.

'He did it very quietly,' said King Winston. 'I would never have suspected a thing. Obviously used really discreet builders.'

Uncle Julian took a step forward and cleared his throat.

'He's collected awful things,' said P.J.

Uncle Julian took a step back.

'I loved those!' said the Moon Hare,

who was standing on his head, trying to lose his hiccups. 'HIC!'

'Where's Foul?' asked P.J. suddenly, noticing that the bird wasn't in his usual place on Uncle Julian's shoulder.

Uncle Julian looked surprised. 'I don't know,' he said. 'To be honest, I didn't notice that he was gone.'

'I don't trust him,' said P.J. 'He gave the map to those pirates and now he's disappeared.'

'I think that Foul is more than he appears to be,' said the Moon Hare unexpectedly, still standing on his head. 'I think that he is not the friend to you, Uncle Julian, that you think he is. HIC!'

They turned to look at the Moon Hare, who, even though he was standing on his head, suddenly appeared to be Very Wise.

It didn't last though.

'My hiccups taste of blue icing,' he said.

'Uncle Julian, why do you think that your map would lead us to Sandra's room?' asked P.J.

Uncle Julian looked uncomfortable.

'Actually,' he said. 'This room used to be mine.'

'Did it?' King Winston was surprised.

'Yes,' said Uncle Julian. 'When I used to live in the castle. Oh, I was a wild one then.'

P.J. tried not to giggle.

'Always up to something daring. That's my secret tunnel, and I collected everything in it.'

'WOW!' said the Moon Hare, turning up the right way.

'Yes,' continued Uncle Julian. 'I had dreams, you know, so many of them, only Mum and Dad didn't. They never dreamed at all. They wanted me to be the king and boring stuff like that, and all I wanted to be was a pirate!'

He began to pace up and down the room.

'Yes! The life of a pirate! Action and Adventure! I used to sneak in and out of

the castle using my secret tunnel; nobody knew what I was up to.'

'Well I never!' said King Winston.

'That's why Elsie and I argued, I suppose,' said Uncle Julian, stopping his pacing to think. 'When I finally left to become a full-time pirate, poor old Elsie had to become the queen. She didn't really want to, you see. I guess that she had dreams of her own . . .'

Uncle Julian looked sad.

King Winston looked sad.

P.J. felt sad too.

She had never really thought of her mum as ever having dreams.

'HIC!' said the Moon Hare. 'Good

news! My hiccups are gone!'

'You just Hicked,' said P.J.

'No, I didn't. $HIC!$'

A sudden noise at the door made them jump.

'They've gone now,' said the Moon Hare.

'Someone is opening the door,' hissed Uncle Julian in a scared voice. 'Do you think it's the pirates?'

It was true; someone was definitely in the corridor outside.

'What shall we do?' asked King Winston, taking hold of Uncle Julian's arm.

'I don't know,' whispered P.J. 'Perhaps

we should hide?'

'HIDE! HIDE! HIDE!' shouted the Moon Hare, and he ran around the room waving his arms above his head.

'Sssh!' squeaked P.J.' and she grabbed hold of him and clamped her hand over his mouth.

'Arm yourselves,' whispered Uncle Julian and he picked up a coat hanger.

'Good idea,' said King Winston, and he picked up an old teddy bear from the bed.

Someone was fiddling about with the lock on the door, they could hear muttering from the other side and then the door swung open.

103

'What are you doing in my room?'

'Sandra!' shouted King Winston in relief.

Sandra entered the room looking furious.

'And what are you doing with Yellow Bear?!'

King Winston's relief disappeared. He looked at the grubby teddy bear that he was holding upside down in front of him.

'Give him to me!'

Sandra was fuming.

'Sandra!' cried P.J., letting go of the Moon Hare and moving towards the dragon. 'Calm down, it's just us!'

Sandra snatched the yellow bear and hugged him tightly. He glared at King Winston, who looked terrified.

'You've made him dirty!' he said accusingly.

King Winston wasn't sure that he could have made the bear look any worse. Its stuffing was coming out and there was none left in its neck, from years of being held lovingly by the throat.

'Your voice can go REALLY loud!' said the Moon Hare to Sandra, impressed.

'You are in my room,' said Sandra, in a calmer and, if they were honest, more worrying voice. 'The Moon Hare I will allow, but you others are UNINVITED.'

'We didn't mean to be here,' began P.J. bravely.

'Do you know that you have a secret

tunnel leading to your room?' asked the Moon Hare, jumping up and down. 'It's fantastic!'

'I do not have a secret tunnel,' said Sandra huffily.

'Oh, but you do! You do!' said the Moon Hare. 'It's through that door over there!' He pointed to the red door.

'That is my wardrobe,' said Sandra.

'You don't wear clothes,' said P.J., even more bravely than before.

'I do,' fibbed Sandra. 'Which is why I need a wardrobe.'

'Have you ever looked inside?' asked P.J.

Sandra gave her A Look.

'I do not need to, smelly girl, for I know that it is a wardrobe. Sometimes I worry that you are not bright.'

'Look!' said P.J., and she opened the red door.

Sandra looked.

'It is a *walk-in* wardrobe,' he said after a pause.

'Yes,' agreed the Moon Hare. 'We walked into your room through it!'

'Moon Hare, let's look at the map again,' said P.J. 'It will tell us where to go next.'

The Moon Hare produced the map. It was even more crumpled than before and there was a splodge of blue icing

smeared across part of it.

'How did you get blue icing . . . Oh, never mind,' said P.J. She turned to the dragon. 'Is there any more news on the other pirate ship?' she asked him.

'Yes, actually,' said Sandra, being unusually helpful. 'All of the pirates seem to have left.'

'They've left?' Everyone held their breath hopefully.

'Yes,' said Sandra. 'They've left their ship and are now on little rowing boats coming to see us.'

'Oh, no!' gasped P.J.

'I had better get back to Elsie,' said King Winston.

'I left Aunty Elsie trying on her favourite crown,' said Sandra. 'The one with all the jewels. Us dragons get rather bored with jewels.'

He gestured to his jewel-encrusted belly.

'We should all make our way back to the Throne Room as quickly as we can,' said P.J. 'The map seems to lead back there anyway.'

P.J. stopped, thinking of what she had just said. She looked at the map again. The route on the paper was very clear. A straight, felt-tipped line leading to the Amazing Maze and then through what they now knew to be the secret tunnel,

ending up in Sandra's room, then back to the Royal Throne Room. That was it.

'Uncle Julian,' began P.J. slowly and carefully. 'Are you sure that this is just like your old map?'

'Yes, I am sure that it is quite the same. Except that it doesn't have as many lines on it as the old one did, or as many details. And the old one didn't have a Lamborghini on it and stuff.'

'Oh, dear,' said P.J.

'Then the pirates' map is wrong,' said the Moon Hare.

'But the pirates have the original map,' P.J. groaned

'Yes but we'll get to the treasure

quicker because we have a Lamborghini,'
said the Moon Hare confidently.

P.J. gave him A Look.

Chapter Eight
A FOUL PLOT

They raced back to the Royal Throne Room to find the large double doors wide open and hanging off their hinges.

The place was in a terrible mess, the wall hangings had been pulled down, tables were overturned, King Winston's beloved chessboard was smashed into tiny pieces and Queen Elsie's throne was upside down.

There were no servants to be found; in fact, the castle seemed to be deserted.

'It wasn't me,' said Sandra quickly.

'No it wasn't. It was me,' said a harsh voice.

'Who said that?' asked King Winston, looking up and down.

'I did.' There was a pause, followed by, 'Oh, for heaven's sake, over here!'

'Where?' asked P.J.

'Over here!' said the voice, sounding frustrated.

They began to look around.

'You're cold . . . cold . . .' said the voice. 'Warmer . . . getting warmer . . . now you're cold again . . . Oh, you're useless at this! **OVER HERE!**'

'Oh, look!' said the Moon Hare,

114

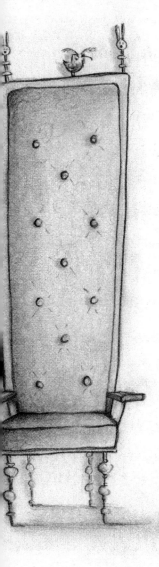

after they had hunted all around the Royal Throne Room. 'It's your budgie, Uncle Julian.'

Sure enough, there was Foul, perched on the back of King Winston's throne, watching them maliciously. 'We didn't see you there, Titchy!' said the Moon Hare, hopping towards him.

'I am not titchy,' snapped Foul.

'Oh, you are!' said the Moon Hare, taking

a tape measure out from his stripy tights
and extending it straight up towards Foul.
'You must only be about ten centimetres
tall.'

'With your shoes on,' added Sandra.

'I am ten-and-a-half centimetres
actually, stupid rabbit,' said Foul
indignantly.

The Moon Hare pressed the red
button on the side of the tape measure
and it reeled in quickly, knocking Foul
down from the back of the throne.

'Oops!' said the Moon Hare.

'DO YOU MIND?' screeched Foul,
climbing back up again.

'Foul,' said Uncle Julian, stepping

forward. 'Do you know what has happened here?'

Foul rolled his eyes.

'Of course I know what happened,' said Foul. 'Because **I DID IT**!'

'What? Destroyed the Royal Throne Room?' said Uncle Julian. 'Oh, why did you do it, Foul, why?'

'Of course I didn't destroy the Throne Room,' said Foul in a tired voice. 'The pirates did that . . .'

'Because you are too titchy,' said the Moon Hare.

'BECAUSE,' said Foul, 'I am the evil genius behind the Cunning Plan. I don't do the destroying part. It's beneath me.'

117

He sniffed in an aloof way.

'What is your plan?' asked P.J., making sure not to call it a cunning one.

'I hoped you'd ask,' replied Foul. He cleared his throat and continued. 'There is a pirate legend that this castle holds a great treasure, a treasure that also has a map revealing its whereabouts.'

He turned to Uncle Julian. 'It didn't take me long to work out that your map was the one the legend spoke of. You were always so careless with it, showing it to everyone.' Uncle Julian looked uncomfortable. 'I had to befriend you to get it, which was **DULL**,' continued Foul unpleasantly, 'but worthwhile, as it

meant that I could steal that map and give it to the pirates!'

'You said that was an accident,' said Uncle Julian looking shocked.

Foul sniggered. 'Don't be stupid,' he said. 'I am the pirates' Captain!'

Everyone gasped.

Foul drew himself up to his full height.

'Definitely only ten centimetres,' whispered the Moon Hare to Sandra behind his paw.

'I couldn't believe my luck when you drew a copy of the map from your memory,' continued Foul. 'A bad copy I might add, and then actually **FOLLOWED**

IT!' He howled with laughter. 'Do excuse me but I enjoy that part!'

'Me too!' said the Moon Hare, and he pulled a flask of tea from his stripy tights, followed by two flowery china cups with matching saucers, a sugar bowl and a small milk jug.

'What are you doing?' snapped Foul.

'Enjoying myself,' said the Moon Hare, passing a cup of tea to Sandra, who took it. 'Do carry on.'

'Yes, well . . .' continued Foul, feeling slightly distracted, 'this got you out of . . . Now what are **YOU** doing?'

He looked at Sandra, who was trying to mime something to the Moon Hare.

'I was asking the Moon Hare if I may have some sugar,' said Sandra. 'I like sugar in my tea.'

'One lump or two?' asked the Moon Hare.

'Three, please,' said Sandra.

'Sorry,' said the Moon Hare to Foul. 'Do go on.'

'AS I WAS SAYING,' said Foul crossly. 'This got you out of . . . Oh, now what?'

The Moon Hare stopped mid-mime.

'I was asking Sandra if he would like a bourbon biscuit,' he said.

'Yes, please,' said Sandra.

'I wouldn't mind one,' said King Winston.

'Me too,' said Uncle Julian.

'WHAT ABOUT YOU, PRINCESS? DO YOU WANT A BOURBON BISCUIT?' screeched Foul furiously.

'Yes, please,' said P.J.

'Do you want to hear my evil genius plan or not?' said Foul sulkily.

'Go on then,' said King Winston.

'Don't know if I want to now,' sniffed Foul.

'Oh, go on,' said the Moon Hare.

'All right, but listen properly,' said Foul. 'Following that rubbish map meant

that you were out of the way and I could let the pirates into the castle and steal the crown!'

'The crown?' King Winston was puzzled. 'Why would you want my crown?'

'Not **YOUR** crown, you idiot!' snapped Foul. 'The queen's crown!'

'The one with the large and incredibly priceless Petulant Diamond on it!' said P.J.

'Yes, well done,' said Foul irritably. 'That's the treasure that the map leads to.' He sighed, looking tired. 'Anyway, the diamond is missing, isn't it? A fact that I discovered only after my crew had taken it and gone back to the ship with the

crown and found . . . this in its place!'

Foul produced the tin foil and sweetie wrapper ball from somewhere inside his oily feathers and threw it down from the back of the throne.

'Elsie's sweetie wrappers!' said King Winston, catching up with the conversation. 'That's a point,' he added, looking around. 'Where is she?'

'The pirates took care of her,' sneered Foul.

'What have they done?' demanded P.J.

'Oh, she's all right,' snarled Foul. 'Annoying woman . . . she's tied up in a cupboard. Now, find the large and incredibly priceless Petulant Diamond

and give it to me!'

'Or what?' shouted P.J.

'Or *this*!' Foul shouted back, and he flew up to the window and, producing a mirror from inside his feathers, he gave a signal – three quick flashes.

'The mirror from his budgie cage!' said the Moon Hare in delight.

'Yes . . . well . . .' Foul looked embarrassed. 'It's useful.'

As he said that they heard an enormous explosion from outside the castle. Foul flew back to the throne and held on tightly with his claws.

The castle shook, knocking them to the floor. Dust and plaster fell from the

Throne Room ceiling. Pulling herself to her feet, P.J. rushed over to the window.

'The pirates have a **GREAT BIG CANNON** on their ship!' she shouted. 'And they've blasted the East Wing of the castle!'

'The East Wing?' said King Winston, joining her. 'But that's my favourite wing!'

The East Wing of the castle was in ruins and thick black smoke poured out from the rubble.

'How could you?' shouted P.J.

'I am a Pirate,' said Foul, pointing to himself. 'You have until bedtime! This castle will be destroyed bit by bit until I have the diamond. I think we'll do the

West Wing next and then the middly bit.'

'That's where my room is!' Sandra was furious. 'I am definitely going to eat you now,' he said. 'Even though you will spoil the taste of my bourbon biscuit.'

He took a step towards Foul.

'I'll be off then,' said Foul quickly, flying up into the air. 'Let me know when you have the Petulant diamond. I'll be with my crew and the **GREAT BIG CANNON**. We may have a barbeque tonight on the beach as the weather is so nice. I would invite you, but I'm thinking that you may be a little busy.'

'Bye bye, Titchy,' said the Moon Hare, waving a paw. 'Close the window on the

way out. If you can.'

'I will deal with you before the end, bunny!' said Foul, and he flew out of the window.

Once out, he turned and pushed it.

'Ha! Ha!' he said triumphantly. 'See, I can close –' but the rest was lost as the window slammed shut.

Chapter Nine
TUNNELS AND
TAPESTRIES

They found Queen Elsie tied up in the wardrobe in her room. She was in a very bad mood. It became worse when they showed her the remains of the East Wing through her window.

'I will roast that nasty little bird,' she growled as they untied her. 'I will pickle him and boil him and scramble him and . . .'

'I'm hungry,' said the Moon Hare.

'Mum, he's after the large and incredibly priceless Petulant Diamond,' said P.J.

'I know he is,' said the queen looking at the mess of the East Wing. 'Luckily, he doesn't know about the secret tunnel.'

'But he does,' said P.J. 'We went down it while he stole the crown!'

'I don't mean Julian's tatty old tunnel,' said the queen, and she took off her dressing gown and put a royal purple cloak over her nightie.

'You know about my secret tunnel?' asked Uncle Julian in surprise.

'Of course I do,' said the queen. 'With

its lime-green carpet and dreadful knick-knacks. Really, Julian, you have no taste.'

'You've been in it?' Uncle Julian looked crossly at his sister.

'Of course,' replied the queen. 'I've been everywhere in this castle, there's nothing that I don't know about it. No, I mean **MY** secret tunnel.'

'*You have a secret tunnel?!*'

'Of course, and don't shout, Julian. Nobody likes a shouter. Everyone has a secret tunnel.'

'I don't,' said King Winston, looking disappointed.

'We will get you one, dear,' said the queen, kissing his cheek. 'You can have Julian's old one.'

'That's my walk-in wardrobe!' said Sandra.

'Oh, yes, of course . . .' said Queen Elsie. 'Well, perhaps you can share mine.' The king looked pleased. 'Or have a corner of it maybe . . .'

'Now you're going back on your offer,' said the king grumpily. 'I will end up with a shelf if I'm lucky.'

'Don't be silly, dear,' said Queen Elsie carelessly. 'I need the shelves for *my* things.'

'ANYWAY!' said P.J., growing

impatient. 'Mum, where is your secret tunnel?'

'It's here, dear,' said the queen, opening a small yellow door in the corner of her room. 'It is where I keep all of my special things. Come along now.'

One by one, they stepped into Queen Elsie's secret tunnel, but when it came to Sandra's turn they had a problem.

Sandra would not fit through the small yellow door.

'I am big boned,' he said.

No one wanted to try to push him through it; it seemed unwise to do that to a dragon. Especially one as chompy as Sandra.

'I will wait here,' he said sulkily. 'Although I think that I am missing out, which isn't fair at all.'

'There is nothing down there anyway, dear,' said Queen Elsie.

'You said your Special Things were down there,' muttered Sandra suspiciously.

'I meant Useful Things, dear . . . like the Hoover and suchlike,' said the queen, disappearing through the door.

'THIS IS FANTASTIC!' came the Moon Hare's voice from inside the tunnel.

Sandra slumped down on the carpet to sulk.

'Please excuse the mess,' said the queen as they entered the tunnel. 'I wasn't expecting visitors.'

The secret tunnel was immaculate. The carpet underfoot was a thick cream and the walls were painted a pale orange. Tapestries hung on every one, separated from the viewer by a thick, red velvet rope.

Some of them were very old and beautifully crafted. They showed portraits of kings and queens, and proud royal horses pulling carriages that had been sewn with a gold thread to catch the light.

'These are lovely!' said P.J. and she meant it, for they were.

'Did you do these?' asked Uncle Julian, thinking perhaps that his tunnel was a bit tatty after all.

'Ooh! No! *These* are the ones that Her Elsiness has done,' said the Moon Hare, who had jumped on ahead. 'Look, that king's got no head!'

They hurried to join him.

'They're lovely,' said P.J., her fingers crossed behind her back. 'But how will this help with the pirate problem?'

'I haven't forgotten them, Petunia,' said the queen, slipping her glasses on to her nose. 'We need to take a good look at all the tapestries. I often find the answer to the most worrying of questions

revealed in them.'

'In the tapestries?' asked P.J.

'In the tapestries, dear,' repeated the queen. 'Whenever I have a worry about a particular Royal Problem, I take a look at my tapestries. Sewn somewhere within them is usually the solution. You just have to look.'

They spread out along the tunnel and began to inspect the tapestries. P.J. couldn't see any clues hidden anywhere in any of them.

The Moon Hare was growing bored. He had started well, every so often he would shout out encouraging things like: **"THIS ONE IS SOOOPER!"**

Or point out things of interest like:
'HORSES!' and 'TRUMPETS!'

After the shortest of time, though, he began to lose interest. He swung on the thick, red velvet ropes until the posts that held them fell, crashing into each other like dominoes. He then began to pick at one or two of the older and more precious tapestries, until the thread started to lift away from the cloth.

'Moon Hare, stop it!' hissed P.J.

'Bored!' said the Moon Hare and he lay on the carpet with his legs in the air, meaning that the others had to step over him to continue.

'Moon Hare!' said P.J. crossly.

The Moon Hare stuck his tongue out at her.

P.J. stepped over him and walked on.

Suddenly, King Winston's voice came ringing out loudly from up ahead. 'Come and look at this!'

The king, looking hopefully for an empty shelf on which to store his things, had walked further than the others. The tunnel had forked and he had taken the turning to the left. This turning led straight on, ending at a flight of stairs, which wound up into darkness. The walls were stone here and the carpet had come to an end, leaving dark red tiles exposed beneath.

King Winston was in the oldest part of the secret tunnel and it had stood undisturbed for many years. They found him staring at a long tapestry that hung on the wall just where the stairs began.

P.J. peered at it.

'It's the Moon Hare!' she said in surprise.

The tapestry that hung before them looked very old, its colours were a little faded, but they could see what definitely looked like the Moon Hare standing in front of some steps that led to a tower.

The tapestry Moon Hare was very

smartly dressed in a gold waistcoat and pantaloons, with red boots, long green gloves and a pointed blue hat worn at an angle between his long ears. He was holding a small wooden box with patterns on each side. The tower behind him was tall and thin and rather like a lighthouse, as it had a window at the top with the brightest light shining from it, its rays sewn from a silver thread that had once sparkled. Over the tower hung the moon, a thin sliver of light against a velvet black sky.

'I'm EVER SO handsome, aren't I?' said the Moon Hare.

'But how could this be?' asked King

Winston. 'How are you in this tapestry hidden away in Elsie's tunnel?'

'I've never seen this tapestry before,' said the queen, puzzled. 'In fact, I've never been in this part of the tunnel before, which is odd. I thought I'd been everywhere down here.'

'Maybe you just haven't *tried* to be in this part of the tunnel before,' said the Moon Hare.

'This is a clue!' said Uncle Julian in excitement. 'Let's go up the stairs!' And he began to run up them.

The others followed, leaving the Moon Hare looking at the tapestry. He smiled a small smile, took the tapestry

from the wall, rolled it carefully and put it into his green stripy tights before bouncing up the stairs two at a time.

At the top was a heavy wooden door. They opened it and found themselves in a small room. It was hexagonal in shape, with a window in each wall.

The room was being used for storage. It held a few rolls of old Christmas wrapping paper, a bedpan, some rope, a tennis racket and a large wooden trunk, which was covered in dust.

To one side of the room was an archway

leading to a balcony, which hung out over the sea. P.J. stepped on to it and looked around.

She was very high up and below she could see the sandy shores of the Little Cove.

Lights twinkled from the beach and she guessed that the pirates were having their barbeque. The smell of burgers and sausages wafted up in the warm evening air.

'I hope that they run out of coal,' said P.J. crossly.

Chapter Ten
MOON MAGIC

'We must have come right through to the other side of the castle,' P.J. told the others as she joined them back in the hexagonal room. 'There's a great view . . . except for the pirates.'

She walked over to the trunk. The dust was thick on its lid and looked like it hadn't been disturbed for years. She wiped some off with her sleeve and saw that there were words carved in the wood underneath:

MARMADUKE & GLADYS

'Mum and Dad!' said Queen Elsie joining her. 'This trunk must have belonged to them.'

'Open it!' exclaimed Uncle Julian, hopping up and down on the spot.

P.J. lifted the rusty latch and opened the trunk. It was empty, apart from a large brown envelope and an old photograph.

Queen Elsie picked up the photograph. 'Mum, Dad and Julian,' she sniffed. 'You always did wear your hair far too long, Julian.' She tossed the

photograph back into the trunk.

'What's in the envelope?' asked Uncle Julian.

Queen Elsie began to open it.

P.J. looked down at the photograph. There was something strange about it, she thought. She bent down and picked it up.

She looked at it.

She looked at the Moon Hare.

The Moon Hare was rummaging around inside his stripy tights. He produced a banana, which he began to eat, throwing its skin on to the floor.

P.J. was just about to tell him to find a bin when Queen Elsie pulled out a letter from the envelope. She read it aloud:

Dear Elsie,

If you are reading this then you have found the hexagonal room, just as we hoped you would. We left the map with Julian, but feared that he would eventually lose it. We had no doubts about you, however, as you were always a clever child, taking after your mother as you do.

We (your father and I) know (oh, your father says hello by the way, he is reading this over my shoulder, which is annoying as he is also eating cheese and onion crisps) . . . Anyway, we know that you never really wanted the responsibilities of being queen and that you felt that Julian should have been king instead. You really mustn't be too hard on him, especially after his bang on the head.

Queen Elsie paused and glanced at Uncle Julian, who looked confused.

Elsie, dear, we know that you had dreams that may not have been fulfilled and so we couldn't think of a better gift for you.

We hope that by having it, you will never wish for more.

Lots of love,

Mum and Dad

xXx

PS. Give our love to Crampyflamppluff.

PPS. We hope that you married that nice Desmond, we liked him.

Queen Elsie hugged the letter against her chest.

'Who is Desmond, dear?' asked King Winston, in what he hoped was a cheery voice.

'What bang on the head?' asked Uncle Julian, feeling for lumps.

'What is the gift?' asked P.J.

Queen Elsie felt inside the envelope and pulled out a small wooden box. It had ornate carvings around each side and on its lid was the Petulant crest and a full moon.

'It's just like the one on the tapestry,' said P.J. 'The one that the Moon Hare was holding.'

'Who's Desmond?' asked King Winston in a slightly crosser voice.

'Open it!' said Uncle Julian, clapping his hands together in delight. 'It might be treasure!'

Queen Elsie lifted the brass latch on on the box and opened the lid.

Inside was an oval-shaped stone. It was smooth and clear and absolutely perfect.

'What is it?' asked Uncle Julian.

'It is a stone,' said Queen Elsie. 'A plain, but rather beautiful stone.'

'It is beautiful!' said the Moon Hare, hopping over to the queen. 'In fact, it's truly FANTASTIC! Hold it up to the moon, Your Elsiness!'

The queen lifted the stone up to the silver light of the moon.

Nothing happened at first. Queen Elsie looked at the Moon Hare, who was staring hard through the open window at the moon above.

Suddenly, the moon seemed to burn bright silver, just for a moment, and then the room was illuminated. The light from the moon hit the stone and it blasted into

153

life, sending a rainbow of colours around the room, smashing the windows and beaming rays of impossible brightness up into the sky.

'TA DA!' shouted the Moon Hare, jumping up and down.

'It's the large and incredibly priceless Petulant Diamond!' shouted P.J.

As the rainbows danced around the room, everyone could feel themselves brimming with happiness and excitement. Any worries that they may have had evaporated in its glow.

King Winston forgot about Desmond, Uncle Julian forgot about his bang on the head, P.J. forgot about the dangerous

pirates and Queen Elsie remembered her dreams.

All of her dreams, every one, and she was filled with a **GREAT HAPPINESS**. They clapped their hands and laughed with joy, dancing about the room.

'THE LARGE AND INCREDIBLY PRICELESS PETULANT DIAMOND!' shouted the Moon Hare, thoroughly enjoying himself.

'So it is,' said a scratchy voice, suddenly cutting harshly through the air.

'Who said that?' said Uncle Julian, looking around.

'Me!' said the scratchy voice.

'Who?' asked P.J.

'Oh, don't start that again,' said the voice. 'I'm over here, on the windowsill. No, not that windowsill ... or that one ... keep going ... Oh, well done.'

There was Foul, sitting, as he had said, on one of the windowsills. The large and incredibly priceless Petulant Diamond seemed to have had no effect on him. He still looked unpleasant and sly.

'I see that you have found it,' he said, smirking. 'We heard the windows shatter and saw the incredible light from the beach. A bit of a giveaway really.'

'You can't have it,' said P.J. crossly, folding her arms.

'It is Mum's. It's always been hers and always will be.'

'I think not, Princess Pooey,' said Foul. 'Queenie knows that if she doesn't give it to me, this room will soon be full of pirates, and the rest of the castle blown to smithereens.'

'Ooh! Lovely!' said the Moon Hare, who still found the prospect of meeting pirates very exciting.

'It will not be lovely,' said Foul crossly. 'It will be very scary indeed.'

'Don't be scared,' said the Moon Hare. 'I'm sure that the pirates won't hurt you. They probably won't even see you because you are titchy.'

'Not me, you fool!' said Foul. 'You! It will be very scary indeed for **YOU**!'

'You can sit on my shoulder if you like,' continued the Moon Hare, jumping up and down. 'Then the pirates will see you and you won't feel titchy. You will feel like a proper parrot.'

'**I AM A PROPER PARROT!**' shouted Foul furiously. 'I mean . . . I'm **NOT A PARROT**, I'm titchy . . . **NO!** I didn't mean that . . .' There was a pause. 'I have a headache now.'

'Maybe you were banged on the head, like Uncle Julian?' asked the Moon Hare.

'I will bang him on the head myself,' said Uncle Julian suddenly, stepping

158

towards Foul. 'You may *Not* have the large and incredibly priceless Petulant Diamond. I will not allow it.'

'NOT ALLOW IT!' shrieked Foul, and then he began to laugh, an unpleasant, throaty laugh that shook his bony body.

'No,' said Uncle Julian very calmly. 'I will not allow you to take the diamond away from Queen Elsie. In fact, I will do everything in my power to stop it.'

'Ha!' said Foul, wiping the tears from his eyes. 'You've never had any power and you've never been able to do **ANYTHING**.'

'You may be right about that, but I can do something now,' said Uncle Julian,

and then he turned to Queen Elsie.
'Could I have the large and incredibly
priceless Petulant Diamond, please?'

The queen looked at him.

'Trust me,' he said.

Queen Elsie thought for a moment
and then handed the jewel to her brother.

'Moon Hare,' said Uncle Julian.
'You're good at jumping. *Catch this*!'

Uncle Julian threw the large and
incredibly priceless Petulant Diamond
high into the air.

Foul flew up quickly but he was not
quick enough. The Moon Hare leaped.

He leaped high into the air.

The large and incredibly priceless

160

Petulant Diamond flew through the archway and out on to the balcony, but the Moon Hare went with it, all the way, catching it neatly in his paw.

As he did so, the door to the hexagonal room flew open and the pirates swarmed in, waving their cutlasses.

'Get them!' screamed Foul as he flew out after the Moon Hare.

Uncle Julian grabbed the rolls of wrapping paper and threw one to King Winston.

Together, they hit the pirates over the head again and again with the rolls. While the surprised pirates were down, the king and Uncle Julian snatched their cutlasses,

which surprised them even more.

Two of the pirates slipped on the Moon Hare's banana skin and P.J. hit them hard with the bedpan.

Queen Elsie slid the trunk into the remaining two pirates and whacked them across the backs of their legs with the tennis racket. While they were down,

she quickly tied them together with the rope.

They then rushed out to the balcony, where Foul had the Moon Hare cornered.

'I've been waiting for this moment,' he sneered. 'You are the most infuriating rabbit that I have ever had the misfortune to encounter. You cannot win, bunny. Give me the large and incredibly priceless Petulant Diamond!'

The Moon Hare blew a raspberry at him.

'Moon Hare!' shouted P.J. and she raced forward, waving her bedpan.

'Give it to me NOW!' shouted Foul, ignoring her.

164

'Shan't,' said the Moon Hare.

'You leave him alone!' P.J. shouted.

Suddenly, Foul produced a rather long and rather sharp-looking sword from beneath his oily feathers.

'Didn't expect that, did you?' he said, still focusing on the Moon Hare, his eyes shining with malice.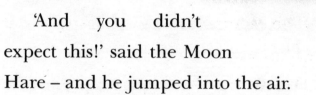

'And you didn't expect this!' said the Moon Hare – and he jumped into the air.

As the Moon Hare jumped, he threw the large and incredibly priceless Petulant Diamond, using all of his strength.

It flew up, up, into the night sky. As it did so, a fierce light blazed from it, lighting up the castle for a moment. On and on it flew, spinning and twisting until it came to a sudden halt.

The large and incredibly priceless Petulant Diamond twinkled in a sky littered with stars.

Foul was astonished.

'**Which one is it?**' he screamed. '**Which one is it?**'

'The shiny one,' said the Moon Hare.

Foul let out a howl of anger. He turned to the Moon Hare.

'**THAT'S IT!**' he cried. '**THAT IS IT! I'm REALLY CROSS NOW**!' He

pointed his sword at the Moon Hare. **'DO YOU KNOW HOW DANGEROUS I AM?'** he screamed.

'I think that I do,' said the Moon Hare. 'But the thing is, Titchy, do you know how dangerous I am?'

Foul faltered briefly, looking confused.

P.J. couldn't be sure, but she thought that the Moon Hare seemed to grow in size. His beautiful brown fur shimmered and for a moment he was all that anyone on the balcony could see.

'I am the MAGNIFICENT MOON HARE!' he said loudly and clearly, his voice ringing out into the night. 'And I

have something that sadly you, Foul, will never have. I HAVE ... FRIENDS!

As he said the word friends, there was a loud

SNAP!

And Foul disappeared in a cloud of oily feathers.

'Now I know that he will upset my delicate stomach,' said Sandra, leaning over the courtyard wall.

The dragon wiped his mouth with a claw and came in to land neatly next to the Moon Hare.

'As I said before, never underestimate a dragon,' said the Moon Hare, bowing low to Sandra. 'You do so at your own risk.'

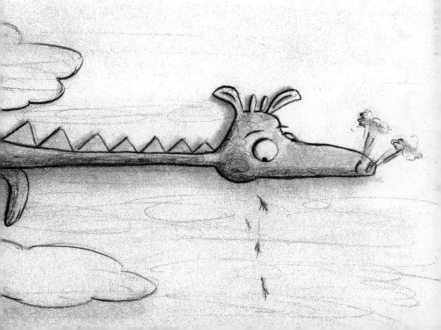

Chapter Eleven
QUEEN ELSIE'S STAR

'Moon Hare, you were *magnificent*!' shouted P.J. and, dropping her bedpan, she rushed up and gave him an enormous hug.

'Yes, I was, wasn't I?' said the Moon Hare. 'And, Sandra, you were ever so dragonish!'

'Of course,' said Sandra. 'I saw that splendid firework display and knew that I was missing out on something lovely, which just won't do. So I flew to where

it was. When I reached here I overheard that little oily thing and he sounded very gloaty as he went on and on, repeating himself over and over. I hope that he doesn't do the same to my digestive system.'

'Have a peppermint, dear,' said Queen Elsie kindly, and she reached into her pocket and pulled out a rather tatty packet of extra strong mints. As she gave one to Sandra, she looked up at the night sky.

The large and incredibly priceless Petulant Diamond was up there, somewhere, although she didn't know where.

'It was lovely, while I had it,' said the queen. 'However, it is just as lovely up there, among the stars.'

'Never mind, my love,' said King Winston, putting his arm around his wife. 'We shall make this our own private balcony, bring a couple of chairs out here and we can look up at it every night.'

'Oh, you don't need to do that, Your Elsiness,' said the Moon Hare, jumping up and down. 'I can get the large and incredibly priceless Petulant Diamond back for you any time that you wish.'

'How will you do that?' asked P.J.

'I am the Magnificent Moon Hare, remember?' said the Moon Hare.

'I am at home in the night-time sky.'

The Moon Hare closed his eyes and put out his paw.

P.J. could see that his lips were moving silently and he was concentrating hard, before slowly, very slowly, she sensed that something was happening in the sky up above them all.

She looked up to see the stars begin to move.

It was difficult to say whether she was imagining it at first, it was so subtle, but after a while, she knew that she wasn't.

The stars *were* moving, and they were moving around a single star, the brightest star of them all. The large and incredibly

priceless Petulant Diamond.

That bright star twitched and wriggled and then it too began to move, only it moved towards the Earth, reluctantly at first but then it picked up speed. Faster and faster it went, until it was racing across the sky.

The other stars leaped around in the darkness, swirling and dancing with excitement, and then there was a single astonishing blast of brilliance illuminating everything.

When it died away, the Moon Hare was left holding a smooth, clear and absolutely perfect stone. 'Your large and incredibly priceless Petulant Diamond,

Your Elsiness,' he said, and he bowed to Queen Elsie.

'Thank you, dear,' she said. Then she stooped down and whispered in his ear, 'Mum and Dad send their love.'

BURP!

'I do beg your pardon,' said Sandra. 'BUUUURP! Oh dear.'

'Your burps are FANTASTIC!' shouted the Moon Hare. 'Do it again!'

'No, don't,' said P.J.

'I'm not doing it on purpose,' complained Sandra. 'BUUUURP!'

'YEAY!' said the Moon Hare.

'Moon Hare!' said P.J. crossly.

'Let me have a go,' said the Moon Hare.

175

'BUUUUUURP!'

'That's disgusting!' said P.J.

'I think that perhaps it is time for some sleep,' said Uncle Julian sensibly.

'Good idea, Julian,' replied the queen. 'Will you be joining us for breakfast in the Royal Throne Room?'

'I should like that very much,' said Uncle Julian.

'BUUUUUURP

'SANDRA!'

'I'M NOT DOING IT ON PURPOSE!' yelled the dragon.

'Come along then,' said the queen, linking arms with King Winston and Uncle Julian. 'Let's leave them to it.'

'Hold your breath,' suggested P.J.

'You hold yours,' said Sandra crossly.

'I mean, to stop your burps,' explained P.J.

'That's for hiccups,' replied Sandra. 'BUUUUURP!'

'That's definitely a burp!' said the Moon Hare, jumping up and down.

'BUUUURPP!'
'MOON HARE!'

Chapter Twelve
CRABS AND CUTLASSES

One evening, not long afterwards, the Moon Hare, P.J. and Sandra were sitting on the sand of the Little Cove.

It was another beautiful evening in Outlandish and the air was warm and smelled of salt and seaweed.

A small crab scuttled past, on its way somewhere.

'Yuck!' shouted Sandra. 'What is that?'

He stood up quickly and shook himself.

'Is it on me?' he asked, spinning around to see. 'Is it?'

'It's a crab,' said P.J. 'It won't hurt you, Sandra, it's more afraid of you than you are of it.'

'I bet it's not,' said the Moon Hare.

'So it should be,' said Sandra, sitting down carefully. 'After all, I am a dragon.'

'It's gone now,' said P.J.

'Nasty snippy thing,' said Sandra. 'With its vicious bitey teeth.'

'Crabs don't have teeth,' explained P.J.

'That one did,' insisted Sandra. 'Big ones.'

'How do they get money from the Tooth Fairy then?' asked the Moon Hare.

'They don't,' said P.J., wishing that the crab had gone in another direction.

'Do they have pillows?' asked Sandra.

'Pillows?' P.J. sighed.

'To put their teeth under,' said the Moon Hare.

'Maybe they keep them in a jar by the bed?' suggested Sandra.

'Why would crabs keep Tooth Fairies in a jar by their beds?' asked the Moon Hare.

'Stoopid,' muttered P.J.

'I hope that the jars have air holes,' said the Moon Hare.

'Moon Hare,' said P.J., thinking it best to change the subject. 'That photograph

that Mum found in the trunk . . .'

'I don't remember,' said the Moon Hare.

'Yes, you do,' said P.J. 'That photograph,' she continued, 'was a picture of King Marmaduke, Queen Gladys and **YOU**, wasn't it?'

'Possibly. I have my photograph taken a lot. I'm very popular,' said the Moon Hare. Then he jumped up. 'Oh, look! The pirates are leaving! Let's go and see them off!'

The pirates, once they had been untied and given a stern talking to from Queen Elsie, had tried very hard to make amends for their bad behaviour.

They revealed the locations of the castle staff. These varied from kitchen cupboards to the downstairs toilet. All of the staff were accounted for except for one footman. The pirates couldn't remember where they had put him, even when they retraced their steps. Suspicion then fell on Sandra, but it was considered unwise to question him too closely.

After that, the pirates were put to work rebuilding the East Wing, including a secret tunnel for King Winston.

This took a while because, after reading a lot of *Tunnel Monthly* magazines, the king kept changing his mind on the decor. Once completed though, he immediately filled it with a giant television set and jars of liquorice allsorts and

disappeared for days at a time.

Sandra, who at first had been used as an escape deterrant by Queen Elsie, had become incredibly fond of the pirates. He made the most of his position as guard by taking every opportunity to talk at length to them on a variety of subjects close to his heart. Subjects like rampaging, devouring and marzipan.

This wasn't as much fun for the pirates, who were terrified of Sandra, and so as not to be eaten agreed with everything that he said, which only made him want to spend more time with them.

'I didn't know that they were leaving today,' said Sandra, feeling disappointed.

'I had arranged a get-together for this evening. I was going to give a talk on my collection of Knights' Helmets, with particular reference to the variety and colour of their plumes.'

'Why do you have a collection of knights' helmets?' asked P.J. as they walked towards the quay.

'I have hobbies,' said Sandra. 'The knights aren't exactly **needing** them any more, if you see what I mean.' He looked at her slyly.

'Oh,' said P.J., wishing that she didn't.

'Ahoy there!' shouted the Moon Hare, jumping on ahead.

He was still wearing his pirate outfit.

185

In fact, he had worn it every day, and to bed too, refusing to take it off even to be washed.

'Ahoy!' said the pirates, taking a small step backwards and holding their noses.

Queen Elsie, King Winston and Uncle Julian were standing on the quayside, waiting to wave the ships off. The queen was feeling the heat and the weight of her crown. The large and incredibly priceless Petulant Diamond had been firmly stuck back in its rightful place, outshining the other jewels surrounding it.

She still hadn't quite forgiven the pirates for attacking the castle and wanted to be sure that they left.

Close up, the pirate ship was impressive. Its beautiful white sails were spotless and its flags fluttered. The brass shone, the gangplank gleamed and the rigging was well rigged.

'Goodbye!' they shouted as they made their way on to the vessel.

'Goodbye! Goodbye!' shouted P.J. and Sandra.

'GOODBYE!' bellowed the Moon Hare, waving his plastic cutlass.

'Goodbye!' shouted Queen Elsie, waving her hand in a distracted way. She whispered to King Winston, 'This seems to be taking an awfully long time, I have things to do.'

'I know,' the king whispered. 'I'm going to miss the start of my television programme.'

'Goodbye! Goodbye!' they both shouted, smiling falsely.

'Are they going?' asked Uncle Julian out of the corner of his mouth.

'I hope so,' said the queen.

The pirates did seem to be taking a very long time to leave. They hoisted the mainsail, although it was already hoisted, and tightened the very tight ropes.

Then they seemed to stand around for a bit.

One of them climbed the rigging.

This caused a lot of excitement, until

188

he came straight back down again.

'Is everything all right, do you think?' P.J. asked the Moon Hare.

'Oh, yes, I expect so,' he replied. 'Aren't they brilliant! Look at them, standing there looking piratey.'

'Is everything all right?' P.J. called out to the pirates.

'Oh, yes!' they called back, looking a little embarassed.

'Are you sure?' P.J. asked, walking up the gangplank.

One of the pirates was pushed forward by the others.

His face was very red and his eyes were downcast. He shuffled his feet

189

awkwardly and fiddled with the brass buttons on his waistcoat.

'It's just . . . well, the thing is . . .' he said, 'we don't really know what to do . . .'

'What do you mean?' asked P.J.

'What he means,' said another, braver pirate, stepping forward, 'is that we don't really know how to make the ship . . . move.'

'You sail it,' said P.J., feeling confused.

'It's that bit that we don't know how to do,' said the braver pirate, nudging the other hard in the ribs.

'I did know once,' said the other pirate, 'but I've sort of forgotten. Captain Foul told us how to do everything.'

'What did he say?' whispered Queen Elsie.

'They don't know how to sail,' the king whispered back.

'They don't know how to sail?' repeated Uncle Julian.

'Oh, good grief!' hissed the queen. 'They can't stay here cluttering up the Little Cove. Julian you go and sail them.'

'I can't do that! I've got my own ship to sail!' spluttered Uncle Julian.

'You need a captain!' shouted the Moon Hare in delight.

'Moon Hare, no!' said P.J.

'Moon Hare, yes!' shouted the Moon Hare, jumping up and down.

'I will come too,' said Sandra. 'For I shall not be left out again . . . although I will not go near the nasty wet water. I will fly overhead and keep you company. The pirates will like that.'

The pirates looked horrified.

'In that case, I'm coming too,' said P.J. 'You'll need someone sensible with you. Mum, Dad, I am going to be a pirate with the Moon Hare and Sandra.'

'Don't be silly, dear,' said Queen Elsie.

'Dad . . .' P.J. pleaded.

'Let her go, Elsie, if she wants to,' said King Winston, looking at his watch. 'She'll have the Moon Hare to look after her. And Sandra, of course.'

They looked at the Moon Hare who was holding one of his long ears straight up whilst trying to look into it with his toilet roll telescope.

'Well, if you put it like that, Winston dear . . .' said the queen.

'But I'm going to look after them!' shouted P.J. 'That's the whole reason I'm going!'

'Can't do any real harm to let her go,' agreed Uncle Julian. 'After all, look at me.'

'I don't think that she should go,' said the queen.

'It's decided then,' said King Winston, thinking that his television programme

would soon be over if they didn't get a move on. 'Take good care of my little P.J.!'

'No!' said P.J. in frustration. '*I'm* going to look after *them*! They can't take care of me, they're useless!'

'You'll be fine, dear,' said Queen Elsie. 'Just do as the Moon Hare says.'

The Moon Hare beamed at P.J.

'Stoopid,' she said, crossing her arms.

'Good luck, pet,' said Uncle Julian happily, patting P.J. on the head.

'I wish that I were going with you . . . but I'm not,' he added hurriedly.

'See you soon,' said the queen. 'We will send you messages via Sandra.'

The pirates led P.J. and the Moon Hare on to the ship.

'Cast the anchor! Weigh the sponge cake and Tally-Ho!' shouted the Moon Hare.

The pirates did as they were told and, amazingly, the ship began to move.

P.J. and the Moon Hare looked across at the quay, moving slowly away from them.

They watched Sandra take to the air, catch up and circle lazily above them, the

195

wind from his wings making the ship rock a little from side to side.

P.J. waved to the party on land, and watched as they grew smaller and smaller. A sudden flash of light from the large and incredibly priceless Petulant Diamond on Queen Elsie's crown illuminated them for a moment, and then they were gone.

'Make yourselves at home,' said a pirate. 'The washing machine and tumble dryer are through there in the utility room.'

He looked pointedly at the Moon Hare's pirate clothes.

'AH-HARRR!' shouted the Moon

Hare in a piratey voice, then he raced very quickly up the ship's rigging.

Sandra hovered close to him and he swung out, holding on to the ropes by one leg.

'Hear me!' he cried and his voice shook the air. 'I am your captain, THE MARVELLOUS, MAGNIFICENT, MAGICAL MOON HARE and I want adventure and excitement, sponge cake with blue icing and lots of FANTASTIC Piratey stuff . . .'

And in the velvet night sky the stars exploded all around him.